# SIX CREEPY SHEEP

Sue Alexander—
There are two creepy sheep who love ewe. —
J.R.E. & S.G.T.

For Tess — J.O.B.

PUFFIN BOOKS
Published by the Penguin Group
Penguin Books USA Inc., 375 Hudson Street, New York, New York 10014, U.S.A.

First published in the United States of America by Caroline House,
Boyds Mills Press, Inc., A Highlights Company, 1992   Published in Puffin Books, 1993

1   3   5   7   9   10   8   6   4   2

Text copyright © Judith Ross Enderle and Stephanie Gordon Tessler, 1992
Illustrations copyright © John O'Brien, 1992

LIBRARY OF CONGRESS CATALOGING-IN-PUBLICATION DATA
Enderle, Judith A.
Six creepy sheep / by Judith Ross Enderle and Stephanie Gordon
Tessler; illustrated by John O'Brien.   p.   cm.
"First published in the United States of America by Caroline
House, Boyds Mills Press, Inc., A Highlights Company, 1992"—T.p. verso.
Summary: Relates in rhyme the adventures of six little sheep who
go trick-or-treating on Halloween night.
ISBN 0-14-054994-3
[1. Halloween—Fiction.   2 Sheep—Fiction.   3. Stories in rhyme.]
I. Tessler, Stephanie Gordon.   II. O'Brien, John, 1953–   ill.   III. Title.
[PZ8.3.E56Si   1993]   [E]—dc20   93-7140   CIP   AC
Printed in the United States of America      Set in Goudy Old Style
The illustrations are done in pen and ink with a combination of watercolors and dyes.

# SIX CREEPY SHEEP

BY JUDITH ROSS ENDERLE
AND STEPHANIE GORDON TESSLER

ILLUSTRATED BY JOHN O'BRIEN

PUFFIN BOOKS

Six creepy sheep said, "Let's trick or treat,"
one spooky Halloween night.

SO...

they wrapped up in sheets.

Then, on little sheep feet, six creepy sheep
went a-haunting

UNTIL...

they passed a passel of pirates, and
one creepy sheep turned tail with a shriek.

Now, on little sheep feet, five creepy sheep
went a-haunting

# UNTIL...

they flew by a flock of fairies, and
one creepy sheep turned tail with a shriek.

Now, on little sheep feet, four creepy sheep went a-haunting

UNTIL...

they happened on a herd of hobos, and
one creepy sheep turned tail with a shriek.

Now, on little sheep feet, three creepy sheep
went a-haunting

UNTIL...

they glimpsed a gaggle of goblins, and
one creepy sheep turned tail with a shriek.

Now, on little sheep feet, two creepy sheep
went a-haunting

# UNTIL...

they whisked by a warren of witches, and
one creepy sheep turned tail with a shriek.

Now, on little sheep feet, one creepy sheep called,

HAPPY HALLOWEEN!